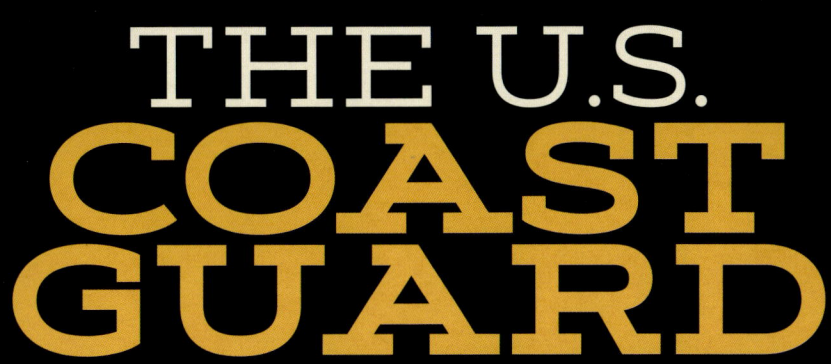

THE U.S. COAST GUARD

INSIDE THE U.S. MILITARY

ROSEN PUBLISHING

BY TANNER BILLINGS

Library of Congress Cataloging-in-Publication Data

Names: Billings, Tanner, author.
Title: The U.S. Coast Guard / Tanner Billings.
Other titles: United States Coast Guard
Description: New York : Rosen Publishing, [2022] | Series: Inside the U.S. military | Includes bibliographical references and index. | Contents: Protecting the Coast – Protecting and Saving – Guard Gear – Coast Guard Careers – Getting the Job Done.
Identifiers: LCCN 2020003425 | ISBN 9781978518612 (library binding) | ISBN 9781978518605 (paperback) | ISBN 9781978518629 (ebook)
Subjects: LCSH: United States. Coast Guard--Juvenile literature.
Classification: LCC VG53 .B55 2022 | DDC 363.28/60973--dc23
LC record available at https://lccn.loc.gov/2020003425

Published in 2022 by The Rosen Publishing Group, Inc.
29 East 21st Street, New York, NY 10010

Copyright © 2022 Rosen Publishing

Designer: Sarah Liddell
Editor: Kate Mikoley

Photo credits: Cover, background used throughout Dakin/Shutterstock.com; p. 4 Craig Lovell/The Image Bank Unreleased/Getty Images; p. 5 Stocktrek Images/Stocktrek Images/Getty Images; p. 7 Chumash11/Wikimedia Commons; p. 10 SAUL LOEB/Contributor/AFP/Getty Images; pp. 12 Ad_hominem/Shutterstock.com; p. 14 Cobattor/Wikimedia Commons; p. 15 POOL/Pool/AFP/Getty Images; p. 18 Joe Raedle/Staff/Getty Images News/Getty Images; p. 19 Fæ/Wikimedia Commons; p. 21 John Lamparski/WireImage/Getty Images; p. 23 Geo Swan/Wikimedia Commons; p. 24 Robert Alexander/Contributor/Archive Photos/Getty Images; p. 25 John_Brueske/iStock/Getty Images Plus/Getty Images; p. 27 Getty Images/Stringer/Getty Images News/Getty Images; p. 28 Drew Angerer/Staff/Getty Images News/Getty Images; p. 31 Hohum/Wikimedia Commons; p. 32 Universal History Archive/Universal Images Group/Getty Images; p. 35 NEIL RABINOWITZ/Contributor/Corbis Historical/Getty Images; p. 37 MENAHEM KAHANA/Staff/AFP/Getty Images; p. 39 (Bruce Melnik) Myself488/Wikimedia Commons; p. 39 (Daniel Burbank) Tom/Wikimedia Commons; p. 42 U.S. Coast Guard/Handout/Getty images News/Getty Images.

Portions of this work were originally authored by Julia McDonnell and published as *Coast Guard*. All new material this edition authored by Tanner Billings.

All rights reserved. No part of this book may be reproduced in any form without permission in writing from the publisher, except by a reviewer.

Printed in the United States of America

Some of the images in this book illustrate individuals who are models. The depictions do not imply actual situations or events.

CPSIA compliance information: Batch #BSRYA22: For further information contact Rosen Publishing, New York, New York at 1-800-237-9932.

CONTENTS

Protecting the Coast 4

Chapter One: Protecting and Saving 6

Chapter Two: Guard Gear 16

Chapter Three: Coast Guard Careers . . . 26

Chapter Four: Getting the Job Done 36

Glossary 46

For More Information 47

Index 48

Words in the glossary appear in **bold** type
the first time they are used in the text.

PROTECTING THE COAST

Countries around the world make plans to keep their citizens safe. A military keeps a country's people and land secure during wartime. It also keeps a nation safe in times of peace, such as during natural **disasters** and accidents. Military forces may also protect citizens from people who break the law.

THE COAST GUARD IS THE SMALLEST OF THE UNITED STATES' FIVE MILITARY BRANCHES. THE OTHER BRANCHES ARE THE ARMY, AIR FORCE, NAVY, AND MARINE CORPS.

The U.S. Coast Guard does just what its name suggests: It guards U.S. coasts and waterways and protects the people who live, play, and work on them. Although the U.S. Coast Guard often serves alongside the other military branches around the world, its main responsibility is the nation's **maritime** needs at home.

CHAPTER ONE: PROTECTING AND SAVING

The first U.S. secretary of the treasury, Alexander Hamilton, didn't want the country to lose money to criminals. To keep that from happening, the Revenue Marine Service was established in 1790. It had 10 ships and would later become known as the Revenue Cutter Service. This early coast guard protected the nation's shores from pirates and foreign navies. It also enforced tax and trade rules and fought **smuggling**.

CUTTER: ANY COAST GUARD SHIP 65 FEET (19.8 M) OR LONGER

THIS PAINTING SHOWS WHAT AN EARLY REVENUE CUTTER MAY HAVE LOOKED LIKE.

As the United States acquired more land and grew bigger, its coastlines grew bigger too. The country also became more involved in international activities. To keep up with this growth, the maritime service's responsibilities had to change. Several departments joined together in 1915 to form the U.S. Coast Guard.

For decades, the Treasury Department oversaw the coast guard during peacetime. In 1967, the coast guard came under the management of the Department of Transportation. After the September 11, 2001, terrorist attacks, the Office of Homeland Security formed. By 2003, the Department of Homeland Security was fully established. That year, it took over control of the coast guard.

CIVILIAN: A PERSON NOT ON ACTIVE DUTY IN THE MILITARY

EXPLORE MORE

DURING TIMES OF WAR, OR AT THE PRESIDENT'S DIRECTION, THE COAST GUARD WORKS UNDER THE DEPARTMENT OF THE NAVY.

ALL IN A NAME

"Coast guardsman" is the official name for any member of the coast guard. The same term is used regardless of a person's gender. "Coastie" and "shipmate" are common nicknames used to refer to people in the coast guard. You may also hear the term "Team Coast Guard." This is used to refer to all types of coast guardsmen—from active duty to civilian—as one group or team. Coast guardsmen serving in different positions or groups may have different kinds of jobs, but "Team Coast Guard" helps us remember they're all part of the same team!

ON JUNE 1, 2018, ADMIRAL KARL L. SCHULTZ BECAME THE 26TH COMMANDANT OF THE UNITED STATES COAST GUARD. COMMANDANTS SERVE TERMS OF FOUR YEARS.

EXPLORE MORE

The leader of the coast guard is called the commandant. This officer is a four-star admiral chosen by the president. The commandant works closely with members of the government and other military branches.

Today, the coast guard functions in two main areas, known as the Atlantic Area and the Pacific Area. The Atlantic Area is on the East Coast of the United States, while the Pacific Area is on the West Coast. These two areas are broken down into nine districts. Districts are further broken down into sectors. Sectors may include cutters, aircraft, and units and teams that can be deployed. Stations located along the nation's coasts work within sectors and use several types of smaller boats for search-and-rescue missions, as well as homeland security duties.

DEPLOY: TO MOVE TROOPS INTO A POSITION OF READINESS

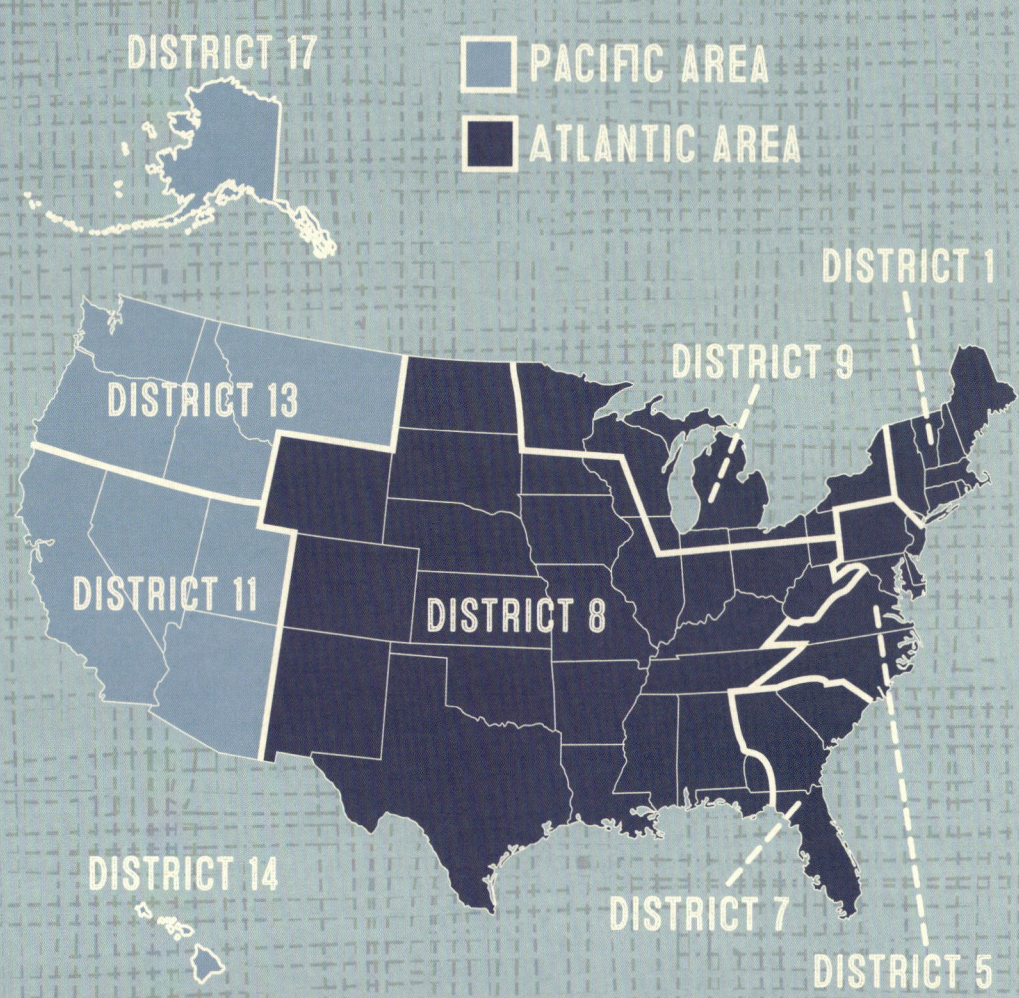

THROUGHOUT HISTORY, THE COAST GUARD DISTRICTS HAVE BEEN REORGANIZED SEVERAL TIMES. TODAY, THE DISTRICTS AREN'T NUMBERED IN ORDER. THERE ARE ONLY NINE DISTRICTS, BUT THE ALASKA AREA IS KNOWN AS DISTRICT 17.

A MEANINGFUL MOTTO

A motto is a short saying that expresses a rule some people choose to live by. The coast guard's official motto is *Semper Paratus*. This phrase is Latin and means "Always Ready." It's a fitting motto for the coast guard because the branch prides itself on always being able to respond quickly and effectively when its services are needed to protect U.S. citizens all over the world. The official marching song of the coast guard is called "Semper Paratus." This is the beginning of the last verse:

> We've been always ready!
> To do, to fight, or die.

On an average day, the coast guard saves 10 lives. During this time, it also performs 45 search-and-rescue cases, stops multiple crimes, investigates accidents, tests boats for safety, and much more.

THE FIRE ON THE *PRINSENDAM* STARTED IN THE ENGINE ROOM. THE SHIP WAS MORE THAN 100 MILES (161 KM) OFFSHORE, BUT THE COAST GUARD WAS STILL ABLE TO RESPOND QUICKLY.

All rescues the coast guard performs, no matter the size, are important. However, the large-scale rescues often seem particularly remarkable. In 1980, a cruise ship called the *Prinsendam* burned in Alaska's icy waters. The efforts of the coast guard's helicopter and cutter crews made sure everyone on board the ship made it out alive. About 520 people were rescued!

When natural disasters strike, the coast guard responds. In 2005, Hurricane Katrina hit the southern United States. It's often considered one of the worst storms to have ever happened in the country. The coast guard saved more than 30,000 lives during the storm. Since its beginnings in 1790, the coast guard has saved more than 1 million lives.

DURING HURRICANE KATRINA, FLOODING CAUSED MANY PEOPLE TO GET STRANDED ON ROOFTOPS. THE COAST GUARD RESCUED MANY OF THESE PEOPLE.

CHAPTER TWO: GUARD GEAR

The coast guard uses a wide variety of aircraft, cutters, and boats. This military equipment is known as assets. As of 2019, coast guard assets included 201 aircraft, 243 cutters, and 1,650 boats.

Large cutters can patrol for months at a time, so crews live on the ship. Though usually found in North American and Caribbean waters, they may cross oceans during international missions. Cutters often keep a smaller boat on board for quick, short trips. National Security Cutters (NSCs) are the largest cutters in the coast guard. They're 418 feet (127 m) long. These are the most advanced of the coast guard's cutters and can complete the most difficult operations.

FAST RESPONSE CUTTERS

All coast guard cutters of the same size and kind share the name of the class they're in. Sentinel-class fast response cutters are 154 feet (47 m) long. Each of these ships is named for a coast guard hero who, through an act of bravery, saved the lives of others. These cutters conduct missions to provide security for coasts, ports, and waterways. They also perform patrols, search and rescues, and help with national defense missions. Commonly, these ships are used to stop illegal drugs from being brought into the United States. They also stop people traveling to the country illegally.

IN 2018, SENTINEL-CLASS FIRST RESPONSE CUTTERS SAVED THE LIVES OF 21 PEOPLE.

Polar icebreakers do just what their name says—they clear paths by breaking up ice in frozen waterways. By doing this, they make sure the United States always has access to places in the polar regions of the Arctic and Antarctic. They bring supplies to stations in remote areas and serve as seagoing laboratories for coast guardsmen and civilian scientists studying the **environment** and other topics. Additionally, icebreakers can go to hard-to-reach places to enforce laws and treaties. These ships are big enough to carry helicopters and can be used for search-and-rescue missions if needed.

FREIGHTER: A SHIP USED TO CARRY AND TRANSPORT GOODS

THE U.S. COAST GUARD ALSO HAS AN ICEBREAKER BUILT FOR THE GREAT LAKES, CALLED THE USCGC *MACKINAW*. IT'S SHOWN HERE GUIDING A FREIGHTER THROUGH ICE.

The *Eagle*, built in Germany in 1936, is the only ship in military service that uses traditional sails. It's a barque. Cadets use this 295-foot (90 m) cutter as a maritime classroom to train and practice skills they'll need in the coast guard. Cadets can travel all over the world while assigned to the *Eagle*.

★ EXPLORE MORE ★

ON THE *EAGLE*, CADETS LEARN IMPORTANT LESSONS ABOUT WORKING AS A TEAM AND LEADING OTHERS. THEY ALSO LEARN BASIC SKILLS FOR HANDLING AND NAVIGATING A SHIP.

BARQUE: A SHIP WITH THREE OR MORE MASTS

CADET: A STUDENT IN TRAINING FOR THE MILITARY

ALL CADETS IN THE COAST GUARD ACADEMY SPEND AT LEAST SIX WEEKS WORKING AND STUDYING ON THE *EAGLE*.

ALL ANIMALS ABOARD!

It's not just human coast guardsmen who contribute to the branch's success. Animals serve in the coast guard too! For years, the coast guard has brought animals on board some of its ships. Sometimes a pet's main duty is to live on board with crew members just to keep their spirits up! Ship **mascots** have included dogs, birds, cats, a pig, and even a bear! Some animals in the coast guard are more than mascots though. Canine explosive detection teams are made up of a dog and their human handler. These dogs go through special training and can find dangerous explosives.

By definition, cutters are a type of boat. However, in the coast guard, a boat usually refers to any coast guard vessel shorter than 65 feet (20 m) long. These tend to operate close to shore and on inland waterways. They may also be attached to cutters. Their missions include search and rescue, and port and coastal security.

THE COAST GUARD'S SMALLER BOATS ARE FASTER THAN THE LARGE CUTTERS AND ARE ESPECIALLY HELPFUL WHEN A QUICK RESPONSE IS NEEDED.

 EXPLORE MORE

THE COAST GUARD MAINTAINS NAVIGATION AIDS THAT BOATERS RELY ON TO STAY ON COURSE AND AVOID DANGER. THESE INCLUDE LIGHTHOUSES, SIGNS, MARKERS, AND **BUOYS**.

Coast guard airplanes are called fixed-wing aircraft. They're able to carry large loads and perform missions that cover long distances. Helicopters are known as rotary-wing aircraft. They manage tight turns and direction changes well. They're also able to take off from and land on the flight decks of larger cutters.

THE COAST GUARD OPERATES LIGHTHOUSES ALL AROUND THE SHORES OF THE UNITED STATES. LIGHTHOUSES ALSO HAVE FOGHORNS THAT WARN BOATERS WHEN IT'S HARD TO SEE THE LIGHT'S SIGNAL.

CHAPTER THREE: COAST GUARD CAREERS

As of 2019, the U.S. Coast Guard had about 56,000 members. There are many ways people serve. The coast guard is made up of active-duty members and civilian workers. Active-duty members include officers and enlisted guardsmen. Newly enlisted members go through eight weeks of basic training. Then, they're appointed to a unit for more specific training. After gaining experience, they start training with their rating's training program where they will receive more instruction for their chosen career path.

ENLISTED: HAVING TO DO WITH MEMBERS OF THE MILITARY WHO RANK BELOW OFFICERS

RATING: A GENERAL JOB AREA IN THE COAST GUARD THAT CONSISTS OF SPECIFIC SKILLS

TO JOIN THE COAST GUARD, YOU MUST HAVE GRADUATED HIGH SCHOOL. IN SOME INSTANCES, A PERSON WHO DIDN'T FINISH HIGH SCHOOL BUT HAS PASSED A TEST CALLED THE GED MAY BE ABLE TO JOIN.

Officers hold leadership positions. Enlisted guardsmen serve as crew members, usually under an officer. A person can become an officer by graduating from the United States Coast Guard Academy, attending Officer Candidate School, receiving a direct **commission**, or advancing through the enlisted ranks.

THE COAST GUARD ACADEMY IS HIGHLY COMPETITIVE, BUT THOSE WHO GET IN DON'T HAVE TO PAY FOR THEIR SCHOOLING AND WILL HAVE A CAREER WAITING FOR THEM AFTER GRADUATION.

AT THE ACADEMY

The U.S. Coast Guard Academy is located in New London, Connecticut. In some ways, it's similar to other colleges. It has academic classes, sports teams, and clubs. However, students at the academy are preparing to become coast guard officers. In addition to regular classes, cadets take part in tough military training and learn how to become good leaders. They also must participate in a sport of some kind. Cadets spend summers on cutters, training new students, or gaining other on-the-job training. After successfully finishing their training at the academy, graduates must complete at least five years of service.

For some members of the service, duties may be different depending on whether it's wartime or peacetime. Since the War of 1812, the coast guard has taken part in many major military actions. This means that coast guardsmen may work in both U.S. waters and international regions. During wartime, the coast guard's main roles are to strengthen and support the navy with service members, ships, and aircraft, and to perform missions requiring skills held by coast guardsmen. Cutters can provide escorts to navy ships making long or risky journeys.

★ EXPLORE MORE ★

THE HIGHEST HONOR AWARDED TO MEMBERS OF THE U.S. MILITARY IS THE MEDAL OF HONOR. AS OF 2019, ONLY ONE COAST GUARDSMAN HAS RECEIVED IT. DOUGLAS MUNRO WAS AWARDED THE MEDAL AFTER HE DIED TO SAVE A GROUP OF MARINES DURING WORLD WAR II (1939-1945).

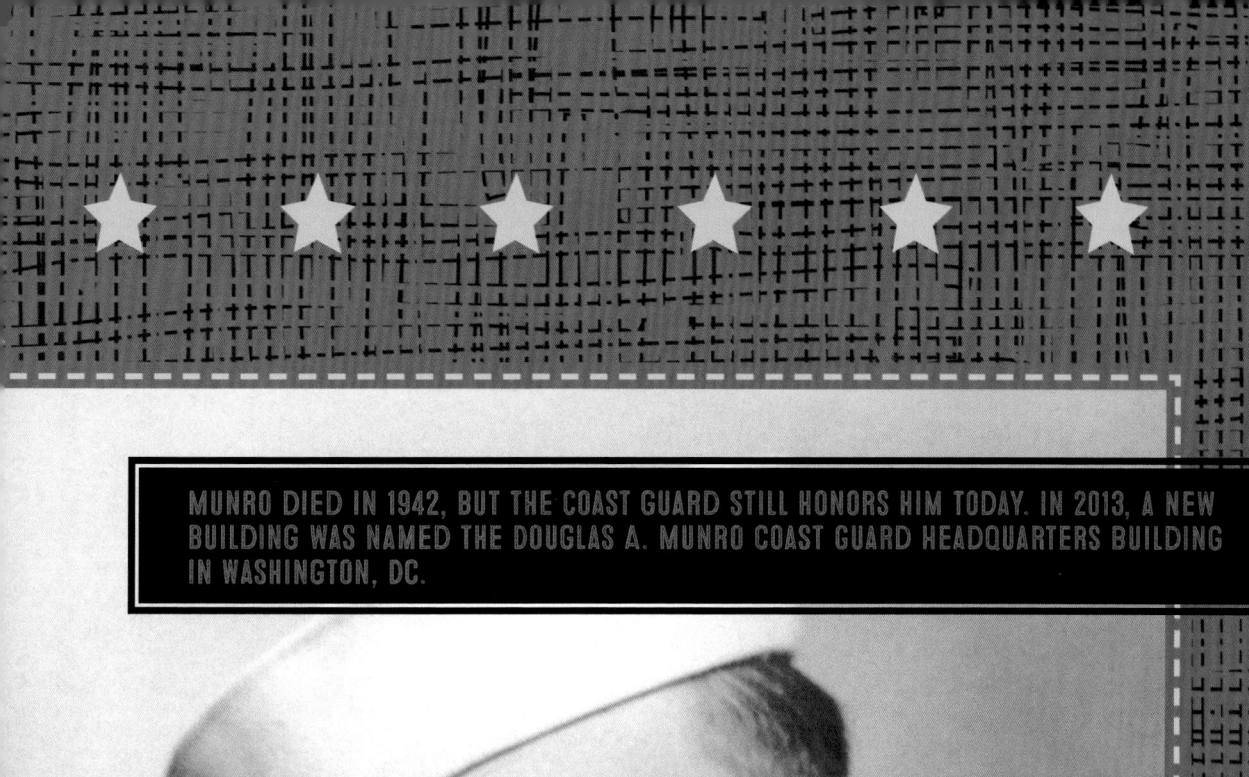

Munro died in 1942, but the Coast Guard still honors him today. In 2013, a new building was named the Douglas A. Munro Coast Guard Headquarters Building in Washington, DC.

One of the most well-known jobs held by members of the coast guard is to perform search-and-rescue missions. The sea can be a dangerous place, and boaters sometimes end up in situations where lives are at risk. Search-and-rescue guardsmen use ships and helicopters to rescue these people at a moment's notice.

RESCUE SWIMMERS HAVE TO BE PREPARED TO GO INTO DANGEROUS WATERS TO SAVE OTHERS.

SAVING THE DAY

Rescue swimmers are considered some of the most **elite** members of the U.S. Coast Guard. They go through training that is both mentally and physically challenging. Only about 75 people go through the training each year, and only about half of them successfully complete it. Rescue swimmers are dropped or lowered from a helicopter to reach someone in trouble. This could be someone lost in dangerous and rough seas, on a cliff, or on a rooftop during a flood. Rescue swimmers' training in emergency medical care helps when rescuing sick or injured ship passengers. They can also help maintain and repair aircraft and its equipment.

Some guardsmen are only in the coast guard part-time. They may hold nonmilitary jobs too. Members of the U.S. Coast Guard Reserve serve two days a month, and an additional two weeks a year. They do many of the same jobs as regular coast guardsmen and can be called upon to work full-time when needed.

 EXPLORE MORE

IN GENERAL, YOU MUST BE BETWEEN AGES 17 AND 31 TO JOIN THE COAST GUARD. THOSE WHO ARE 17 NEED PERMISSION FROM THEIR PARENT. RESERVISTS CAN BE BETWEEN 17 AND 40.

AUXILIARY: REFERRING TO CIVILIAN VOLUNTEERS WHO PROVIDE SUPPORT TO A MILITARY WHEN NEEDED

AUXILIARY MEMBERS PROMOTE BOATING SAFETY AND TRAINING. WHEN NEEDED, THEY ALSO PERFORM RESCUES.

Some employees of the coast guard are civilians who have no active-duty experience but perform jobs that support coast guard operations. This includes lawyers, engineers, and other experts.

The United States Coast Guard Auxiliary is made up of former service members and civilians who volunteer their time to educate **recreational** boaters and watch over seaside communities. Today, about 26,000 people serve in the auxiliary.

CHAPTER FOUR: GETTING THE JOB DONE

Coast guardsmen work hard to help people living around the United States, and even in other parts the world. In 2010, the coast guard brought aid to victims of a terrible earthquake in Haiti. In 2019, it made efforts to help when a hurricane struck the Bahamas. Man-made problems, such as major oil spills, often require fast responses from the coast guard too.

★ EXPLORE MORE ★

Women began serving officially with the coast guard as lighthouse keepers in the 1830s. During World War II, women were hired as civilian employees in the Women's Reserve, or SPARS. In 1973 women could finally become active-duty members.

The Coast Guard works with other military branches to help people during disasters. Shown here, members of the Army and Coast Guard worked together during Hurricane Katrina.

COAST GUARD IN SPACE

It's not unusual for an astronaut to have served in the military. However, as of 2019, only two members of the U.S. Coast Guard have gone on to become astronauts. These two people are Commander Bruce Melnick and Captain Daniel Burbank, both pilots and Coast Guard Academy graduates. Chosen by NASA to join the program, they trained for several years. Each spent hundreds of hours in space. They've said that their time in the coast guard helped them learn important lessons that carried over into their duties in space.

STEWARDSHIP: THE JOB OF PROTECTING SOMETHING. IT OFTEN REFERS TO THE RESPONSIBILITY FOR ENVIRONMENTAL QUALITY SHARED BY ALL THOSE WHOSE ACTIONS AFFECT THE ENVIRONMENT.

The main goal or mission of the U.S. Coast Guard is to ensure the country's maritime safety, security, and stewardship. Maritime safety means keeping people safe at sea. One way this is done is by conducting search-and-rescue operations to save people and property in danger at sea. Other marine safety duties include looking into accidents, inspecting ships, and educating Americans through boating safety programs.

BRUCE MELNICK AND DANIEL BURBANK, SHOWN HERE, ARE THE FIRST TWO MEMBERS OF THE U.S. COAST GUARD TO HAVE BECOME ASTRONAUTS.

MILITARY PHONETIC ALPHABET

A: ALPHA	N: NOVEMBER
B: BRAVO	O: OSCAR
C: CHARLIE	P: PAPA
D: DELTA	Q: QUEBEC
E: ECHO	R: ROMEO
F: FOXTROT	S: SIERRA
G: GOLF	T: TANGO
H: HOTEL	U: UNIFORM
I: INDIA	V: VICTOR
J: JULIET	W: WHISKEY
K: KILO	X: XRAY
L: LIMA	Y: YANKEE
M: MIKE	Z: ZULU

TO AVOID CONFUSION, MEMBERS OF THE COAST GUARD AND OTHER BRANCHES OF THE MILITARY USE WORDS TO REPRESENT LETTERS WHEN SPEAKING OVER THE RADIO. THIS IS CALLED THE PHONETIC ALPHABET.

BEACON: A STRONG LIGHT USED TO HELP GUIDE SHIPS THAT CAN BE SEEN FROM FAR AWAY

Maritime stewardship means protecting the marine environment and its resources. The coast guard enforces fishing laws, responds to accidents that could harm the ocean, works to protect **endangered** species, and prevents water pollution. It also keeps waterways free of ice for ships traveling through the area and makes sure buoys and beacons work properly.

MEMBERS OF THE U.S. COAST GUARD SOMETIMES TAKE PART IN DEMONSTRATIONS WHERE THEY SHOW OFF THEIR SKILLS TO THE PUBLIC.

Maritime security involves keeping U.S. ports and waterways safe and responding to attacks made on them. It's the coast guard's duty to enforce treaties, agreements, and laws on the sea. Coast guardsmen are trained to keep illegal drugs from coming into the country. They also stop people from traveling to the United States without proper **documentation**. Maritime security also includes serving with and supporting the U.S. Navy around the world during war and in times of peace.

CRISIS: A TOUGH AND DANGEROUS SITUATION THAT REQUIRES SERIOUS ATTENTION

PORT SECURITY UNITS

Port security units (PSUs) protect important waterside areas and assets such as piers, harbors, and high-value ships all over the world. The people who make up PSUs are members of the coast guard reserve. However, unlike other reserve units, PSUs are commonly deployed overseas when needed. PSUs can deploy within 96 hours of getting orders. They can be fully operational within 24 hours of arriving at their new location and carry enough supplies to support themselves for 30 days. PSUs have helped the navy in many times of crisis.

WHERE ARE THE PORT SECURITY UNITS?

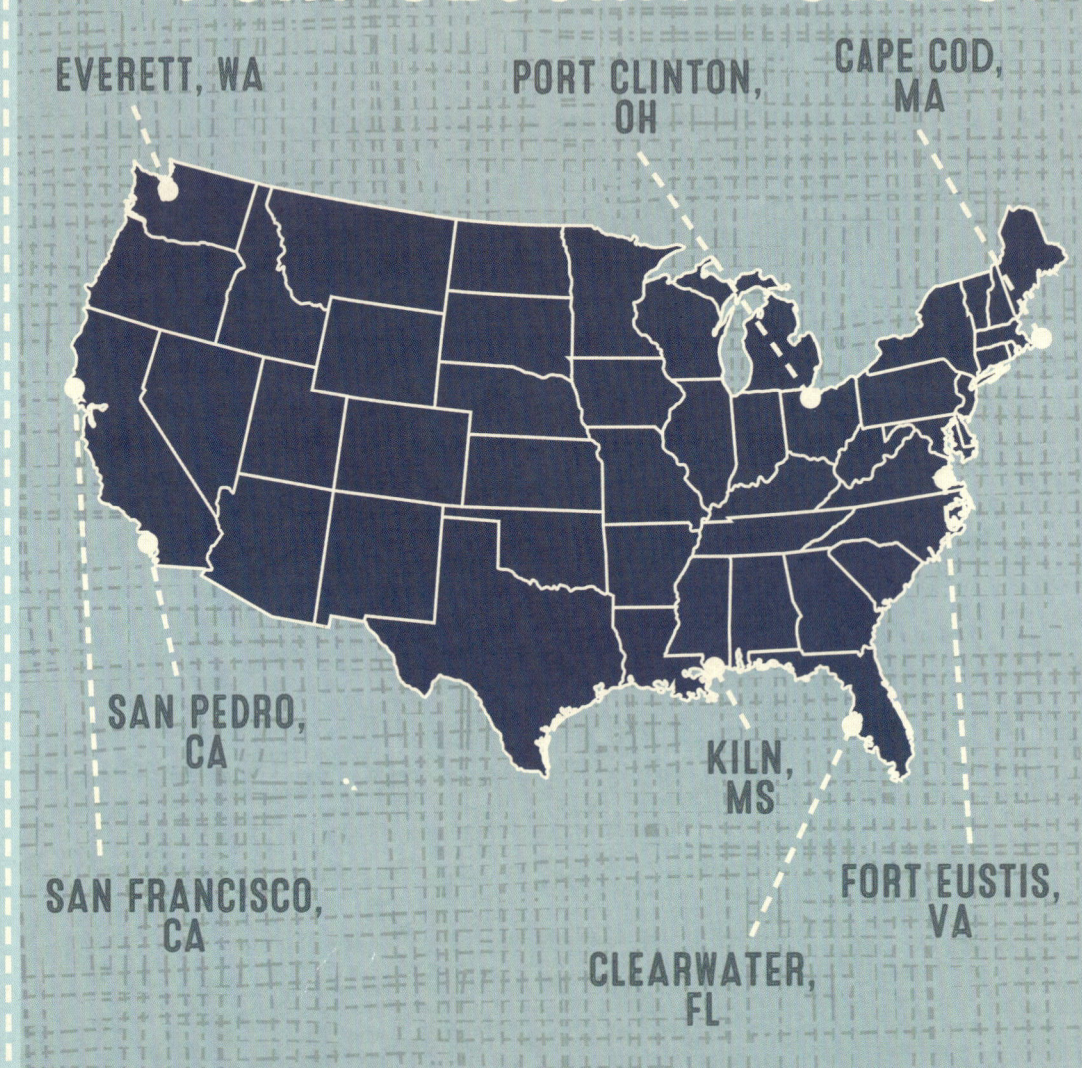

EVERETT, WA

PORT CLINTON, OH

CAPE COD, MA

SAN PEDRO, CA

KILN, MS

SAN FRANCISCO, CA

FORT EUSTIS, VA

CLEARWATER, FL

PSUs ARE LOCATED ON EIGHT COAST GUARD BASES AROUND THE UNITED STATES.

44

To meet the nation's needs, the U.S. Coast Guard regularly inspects and improves its ships and designs. As better technology becomes available, it builds new assets to help the country advance. The service also constantly trains guardsmen to respond to threats on U.S. citizens and the environment.

The coast guard's core values are "Honor, Respect, and Devotion to Duty." Honor means behaving morally and being loyal. Respect means treating people fairly and kindly. Devotion to duty means being committed and proud of your service. By keeping these values in mind as it moves forward, the U.S. Coast Guard can stay true to its beginnings and continue to grow as an important tool for the United States, its citizens, and people around the world.

★ **EXPLORE MORE** ★

PEOPLE WHO ENTER THE COAST GUARD ARE **DEDICATED** TO SERVING THEIR NATION, HONORING THEIR DUTY TO PROTECT THE PEOPLE, AND REMAINING COMMITTED TO EXCELLENCE.

GLOSSARY

buoy A floating object used to guide ships or mark a place in the water.

commission A document giving someone a position of high rank in the military.

dedicated Having strong support or loyalty toward a cause.

disaster An event that causes much suffering or loss.

documentation Documents, records, and other materials used to make something official.

elite The best of a class.

endangered In danger of dying out.

environment The natural world in which plants or animals live.

maritime Relating to the sea or sailing.

mascot A person, animal, or object used to represent a team or group of people.

recreational Something done for pleasure or relaxation.

smuggling Importing or exporting goods illegally.

FOR MORE INFORMATION

BOOKS

Abdo, Kenny. *United States Coast Guard*. Minneapolis, MN: Abdo Zoom, 2019.

Polacco, Patricia. *Remembering Vera*. New York, NY: Simon & Schuster Books for Young Readers, 2017.

Sutter, Marcus. *Heroes on the Home Front*. New York, NY: HarperFestival, 2020.

Toth, Vince. *My Sister Is in the Coast Guard*. New York, NY: PowerKids Press, 2016.

WEBSITES

Go Coast Guard
www.gocoastguard.com
Find out more about the different jobs, requirements, and benefits of joining the U.S. Coast Guard.

United States Armed Forces
www.ducksters.com/history/us_government/united_states_armed_forces.php
Read about the different branches of the armed forces here.

United States Coast Guard
www.uscg.mil
Learn more about the coast guard on its official military website.

Publisher's note to educators and parents: Our editors have carefully reviewed these websites to ensure that they are suitable for students. Many websites change frequently, however, and we cannot guarantee that a site's future contents will continue to meet our high standards of quality and educational value. Be advised that students should be closely supervised whenever they access the internet.

INDEX

A
air force, 5
army, 5, 37

B
Burbank, Captain Daniel, 38, 39

C
Coast Guard Academy, 21, 28, 29, 38
Coast Guard Auxiliary, 35
coast guard reserve, 34, 43
commandant, 10, 11
cutter, 6, 7, 11, 14, 16, 17, 18, 20, 23, 24, 25, 29, 30

D
district, 11, 12

G
guardsman, 9, 18, 22, 26, 28, 30, 32, 34, 36, 42, 45

H
Hamilton, Alexander, 6

M
marine corps, 5, 30
Melnick, Commander Bruce, 38, 39
motto, 13
Munro, Douglas, 30, 31

N
navy, 5, 30, 42, 43

P
port security unit, 43, 44

S
Schultz, Admiral Karl L., 10

W
Women's Reserve (SPARs), 36